The Teeny Tiny Teacher

The Teeny Tiny Teacher

A TEENY TINY GHOST STORY
ADAPTED A TEENY TINY BIT

BY **STEPHANIE CALMENSON**
ILLUSTRATED BY **DENIS ROCHE**

Scholastic Inc.
New York Toronto London Auckland Sydney

ISBN 0-590-37124-X

Text copyright © 1998 by Stephanie Calmenson.
Illustrations copyright © 1998 by Denis Roche.
All rights reserved. Published by Scholastic Inc.

SCHOLASTIC and associated logos are trademarks and/or registered trademarks of Scholastic Inc.

12 11 10 9 8 7 6 5 4 3 2   8 9/9 0 1 2 3/0

Printed in the U.S.A.   14

First Scholastic paperback printing, September 1998

The display face was set in Gill Sans Extra Bold. • The text was set in Gills Sans Regular. The illustrations are gouache. • Book design by Marijka Kostiw

To Nina and Ben —S.C.

For Giles and Eliza —D.R.

Once upon a time, there was
a teeny tiny teacher who taught
in a teeny tiny school
in a teeny tiny town.

One teeny tiny morning,
after taking the teeny tiny attendance

and singing teeny tiny morning songs,

the teeny tiny teacher said,
"Who would like to take a teeny tiny walk?"
"Me!!!" called all the teeny tiny students
in their teeny tiny voices.

The teeny tiny students
put on their teeny tiny coats
and their teeny tiny hats.
They made two teeny tiny lines,
holding teeny tiny hands,
as they walked to a teeny tiny park.

At the teeny tiny park
they found many teeny tiny things.
Teeny tiny leaves. Teeny tiny sticks.
Teeny tiny rocks. Teeny tiny feathers.
And the teeny tiny teacher found a teeny tiny bone.

"I will save this teeny tiny bone
for our teeny tiny science lesson,"
said the teeny tiny teacher to her teeny tiny self.
She put the teeny tiny bone into her teeny tiny pocket.

When the teeny tiny class got back
to their teeny tiny room,
they hung their teeny tiny coats
and their teeny tiny hats in the teeny tiny closet.
The teeny tiny teacher forgot all about
the teeny tiny bone in her teeny tiny pocket.
"Who is ready for a teeny tiny snack?"
asked the teeny tiny teacher.
"We are!!!" said all the teeny tiny students.

While the teeny tiny teacher
was filling teeny tiny cups with juice,
a teeny tiny voice whispered,

The teeny tiny teacher smiled,
thinking a teeny tiny student was
playing a teeny tiny trick on her.
"Someone is being a teeny tiny bit silly,"
said the teeny tiny teacher.
Then she handed out the teeny tiny cups of juice
and passed around teeny tiny cookies.

The teeny tiny students were enjoying
their teeny tiny snack when the teeny tiny voice said
a teeny tiny bit louder,

GIVE ME MY BONE!

The teeny tiny students were a teeny tiny bit frightened!
They spilled their teeny tiny cups of juice
and dropped their teeny tiny cookies
all over the teeny tiny floor!

"Someone is being more than a teeny tiny bit silly now," said the teeny tiny teacher, with her teeny tiny hands on her teeny tiny hips. "Teeny tiny students who have something to say must raise their teeny tiny hands."

A teeny tiny student raised
her teeny tiny hand and said,
"The teeny tiny voice came
from our teeny tiny closet!"
"Teeny tiny closets do not talk,"
said the teeny tiny teacher.
Then she helped her teeny tiny students
clean up the teeny tiny room.

When the teeny tiny room was a teeny tiny bit tidy,
the teeny tiny teacher said,
"Who would like to help me write a teeny tiny story
about our teeny tiny walk?"
"Me!!!" said all the teeny tiny students.
They were taking turns telling the teeny tiny teacher
what to write when the teeny tiny closet
started to *shake* and *rattle* and the teeny tiny voice
called out a teeny tiny bit louder.

Now the teeny tiny students
and the teeny tiny teacher were
a teeny tiny bit frightened!
They hid under their teeny tiny desks!

They had been hiding just a teeny tiny time
when the teeny tiny voice called out
a teeny tiny bit louder than before,

GIVE ME MY BONE!

This made the teeny tiny teacher
and her teeny tiny students
a teeny tiny bit *more* frightened,
so they hid a teeny tiny bit farther
under their teeny tiny desks.
They were shivering and shaking
a teeny tiny bit when
the teeny tiny voice called again
a teeny tiny bit louder.

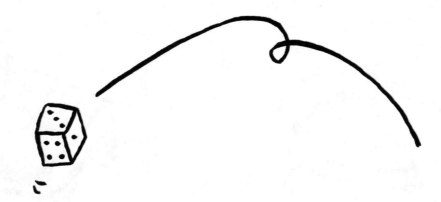

The teeny tiny teacher was not about
to let a teeny tiny voice frighten her
teeny tiny students another teeny tiny minute,
so she popped up from her teeny tiny desk and
shouted in her loudest teeny tiny voice,

TAKE IT!

After that, the teeny tiny teacher
and her teeny tiny students never heard
the teeny tiny voice again.

And that is the teeny tiny end.